Fun & Funny
APRIL FOOL'S
Jokes & Riddles

D.J. Arneson

Illustrated by
Hilde Antonsen

TOR

A TOM DOHERTY ASSOCIATES BOOK
NEW YORK

FUN AND FUNNY APRIL FOOL'S JOKES AND RIDDLES

A Tor Book
Published by Tom Doherty Associates, Inc.
175 Fifth Avenue
New York, N.Y. 10010

Tor® is a registered trademark of Tom Doherty Associates, Inc.

Cover and interior art by Hilde Antonsen

ISBN: 0-812-51642-7

First edition: April 1992

Printed in the United States of America

0 9 8 7 6 5 4 3 2

April Fooler—Ghostbuster

Mention the subject of ghosts while talking with a friend.

Tell your friend you aren't afraid of ghosts because you know how to get rid of them.

When your friend asks you to prove it, put your hand to your forehead. Pretend to concentrate very hard. Then, quickly say out loud, "GO AWAY GHOSTS!"

Slowly look around. Ask your friend, "Do you see any ghosts?"

When your friend says "no," you say, "See, it works!"

Joe: Why should you be careful when you tell
    jokes to ghosts?
Moe: They might laugh themselves to life.

Knock, knock.
Who's there?
Clark.
Clark who?
Clark clark, I'm a chicken.

Mr. Heap: Junior is spoiled rotten.
Mrs. Heap: He isn't spoiled. He just needs his
    diaper changed.

Jon: Why aren't you afraid to go out after dark?
Ron: Because after dark, it's light.

Willie chewed a wad of gum;
he stored it briefly on his thumb.
Teacher said, "No gum in here."
So Willie stuck it in his ear.

Bony Bill: What do skeletons say when they
    shake hands?
Ribby Robin: Give me some skin.

New Scuba Diver: How do you know if there
   are ghosts in old sunken ships?
Scuba Teacher: I just look for their boobles.

What do you get when you cross a sheep with a
gorilla?
   A baaa-*boon.*

Spaceship Pilot: We're running low on fuel, sir.
Spaceship Captain: Quick! Turn the calendar to April.
Spaceship Pilot: What good is that, sir?
Spaceship Captain: Didn't they teach you that April 1st is April Fuel's Day?

Knock, knock.
Who's there?
Seymour.
Seymour who?
Seymour if you open the door.

Astronomy Teacher: Who knows why the night sky is black?
Student: It's full of star dust.

Baker's Apprentice: Oh, oh! I dropped a pumpkin into the bread dough. Now it's ruined.
Baker: No, it's not. We'll just call it pumpkinickel bread.

What do you get when you cross King Kong with Ronald MacDonald?
    A really BIG Mac.

Why do elephants eat mothballs?
  To keep moths out of their trunks.

Knock, knock.
Who's there?
Dwayne.
Dwayne who?
Dwayne de tub, I'm d'wowning.

What's black and blue and goes around the
Earth?
  The sky.

Doctor: What should I wear to the formal dinner
        tonight?
Doctor's Wife: Why, your doxedo, of course.

History Teacher: Name two famous explorers.
Billy: How could they be famous if they don't
       already have names?

What do you get if you cross a garden hose with
a crocodile?
  An irrigator.

5

What do you call Superman between two slices of bread?
A hero sandwich.

First Detective: My hardest job was finding a
    needle in a haystack.
Second Detective: That's nothing. I had to find
    the where wolf and the invisible man.

Teacher: Where is the new student who sat next to you yesterday?

Student: Mike Howe is sick.

Teacher: I'm sorry to hear about your cow, but I asked about the new student.

Knock, knock.
Who's there?
Isadore.
Isadore who?
Isadore locked?

What's green and blue at the same time?
    A *sad pickle.*

What do you get if you cross a chicken with an elephant?
    I don't know, but you'd have a lot of trouble getting it into a frying pan.

First Gardener: I crossed a tree with a lollipop. What should I call it?

Second Gardener: A sap sucker.

Horseback Rider: Where can I tie up my horse?
Traffic Cop: Park him on Mane Street.

What do you call a reindeer with 100 legs?
  A Santapede.

Knock, knock.
Who's there?
Dustin.
Dustin who?
Dustin the air. You should close the door.

Street Sweeper: Did it hurt when the street lamp
    fell on your head?
Street Cleaner: No, it was a light pole.

Teacher, teacher, oh so nice.
Always follow his advice.
But when he says you get an F,
smile at him and say you're deaf.

Farmer: What happens when a sheep scratches
    its back?
Mary: Fleas flee fluffy fleece.

8

Knock, knock.
Who's there?
Heywood.
Heywood who?
Heywood you please open the door?

Gilmore Goblin: Why are you wearing a
    Kleenex instead of a sheet?
Gomer Ghost: I have a runny nose.

Teacher: How would you define "Pie in the
    Sky," Rachel?
Rachel: The bakery blew up.

Jeff: What do you call a bath in cold water?
Mutt: A *brrrr'd* bath.

What's worse than a turtle with claustrophobia?
    An elephant with hay fever.

Knock, knock.
Who's there?
Murry Lee.
Murry Lee who?
Murry Lee we roll along.

Knock, knock.
Who's there?
Jess.
Jess who?
Jess me.

Teacher: What is the sum of 3 plus 7 plus 4 plus 15?
Student: Some is 10 and the rest is left over.

Salesman (*at door*): Is your mother at home?
Martha: Yes.
Salesman: May I talk to her?
Martha: She's not here.
Salesman: But you said she was at home.
Martha: She is. This isn't our house.

Knock, knock.
Who's there?
Raoul.
Raoul who?
RRRRaoull! I'm the Wolfman!

What telephone company do canaries use for making bird calls?
   A *Tweet & Tweet.*

Knock, knock.
Who's there?
Shelby.
Shelby who?
Shelby coming 'round the mountain.

What do you get when you cross a chair with a pot of honey?
  Sticky buns.

April Fooler—Eggspert

You can play this April Fooler whenever there is an egg around. It can be on your plate, in the refrigerator or at the store.

Study the egg for a long time. Say, "Very interesting." Turn to a friend and say, "I can tell exactly where this egg came from."

When your friend says to prove it, place your hand on your forehead. Stare at the egg. Pretend to concentrate very hard. Then suddenly announce, "This egg came from a *chicken!*"

Knock, knock.
Who's there?
Hugh.
Hugh who?
Hugh hoo, it's me.

Mother Ghost: How will baby ever learn to float in the air without falling down?
Father Ghost: We'll put him in training sheets.

Noah: What kind of fish cooks its breakfast?
Jonah: The one with pancake flippers.

Geography teacher: What's the name of the world's best known waterfall?
Claude: Rain.

Farmer: What do you call a fast-eating ghost turkey?
Frank: A gobblin' goblin gobbler.

Invisible Woman Looking into her Closet: "How nice. I have absolutely nothing to wear."

April Fooler—Long distance voice

Tell a friend you can talk to anyone in a normal voice, even if the person is miles away.

When your friend asks you to prove it, say, "Sure. Who do you want me to talk to?"

When your friend says the person's name, close your eyes. Pretend to concentrate. Shake your head. Act as if the trick is harder than you thought. Suddenly say, "I can do it!" Open your eyes and say, "Quick! What's the person's telephone number?"

Knock, knock.
Who's there?
Althea.
Althea who?
Althea later, alligator.

Weird Scientist: I just crossed a chicken with a
    centipede.
Strange Assistant: Yahoo! Drumsticks for
    everyone!

Abdul: What flies over the desert on Halloween?
Omar: The sand-witch.

Knock, knock.
Who's there?
Lucy Ann.
Lucy Ann who?
Lucy Ann Charlie Brown.

Knock, knock.
Who's there?
Cain?
Cain who?
Cain you come out to play?

Why did the elephant wear sunglasses?
   *With all the stupid elephant jokes going
   around, it didn't want to be recognized.*

Knock, knock.
Who's there?
Fido.
Fido who?
Fido I have to wait out here?

April Fooler—Two-headed Monster

To prepare: Hide two coins in one hand.

Pretend you see something very small flying around the room. Get a friend's attention by saying, "Wow! Look at that awful creature!" Your friend won't see anything, of course.

When your friend's interest is really high, grab the air with your empty hand. Pretend you caught the "thing." Cup both hands and peek inside. Say, "Yech! I see two heads and two tails!"

When your friend asks to see what you caught, say no. Say it's too ugly to show. Finally give in. Say, "Well, if you insist."

Open your hands slowly and show the two coins. Say, "I told you. Two heads and two tails!"

Sun Bather: Why can't I sing on the beach?
Lifeguard: You'll get a shore throat.

Knock, knock.
Who's there?
Missouri.
Missouri who?
Missouri loves company.

What is true and false about dogwood trees at
the same time?
   A dogwood tree has no bark.

Pet Lover: If Burmese cats come from Burma
      and Siamese cats come from Siam, where
      do copy cats come from?
Bird Brain: From the Xerox machine.

Lumberjack: What will happen if I pour soda
      water on an oak tree?
Lumber Jim: You'll get pop acorn.

Sniffles: Who can cure my hay fever?
Nurse: The Lawn Doctor.

April Fooler—The Clever Coin

To prepare: You will need a coin for this April Fooler.

Show a friend an ordinary coin. Tell your friend he or she can have it if he or she can pick it up.

Place the coin about two feet from the base of a wall.

Tell your friend to stand against the wall, facing the coin. Say, "All you have to do is bend over and pick up the coin. You must keep your feet flat on the floor and your heels touching the wall."

Your friend will not be able to pick up the coin. Try it yourself to see why.

Put the coin back into your pocket. Now tell your friend that you can pick up a coin from the identical spot.

Ask your friend for a coin. Place your friend's coin on the same spot you put the first coin. Ask, "Is this the identical spot?" When your friend agrees, bend down and pick up the coin. Of course, when you pick up the coin, don't stand against the wall. Put your friend's coin into your pocket. Smile and say "Fooled you!"

Knock, knock.
Who's there?
Murry.
Murry who?
Murry up or we'll be late.

What goes up but never comes down?
   The up escalator.

Knock, knock.
Who's there?
Gillette.
Gillette who?
Gillette the cat out?

Robber: What holds up banks and never gets
        caught?
Cop: Walls.

Knock, knock.
Who's there?
Thurston.
Thurston who?
Thurston for a glass of water.

Ace: What do you get when you cross peanuts
with golf balls?
Grace: Peanut putter.

Exterminator: Why can't I bait my mousetraps
with peanuts?
Animal Lover: You might catch an elephant.

Weird Scientist: I crossed a cow with a
newspaper last night.
Strange Assistant: What did you get?
Weird Scientist: The evening moos.

First Parachute Jumper: Help! My parachute
won't open.
Second Parachute Jumper: Catch a ride with
someone going the other way.

Knock, knock.
Who's there?
Justin.
Justin who?
Justin time.

Aunty: I understand you love going to school.
Herky: I also love going home. It's the part in
the middle I can't stand.

Television Announcer: What are the chances of
a shower tonight?
Weatherman: Go ahead and take one if you
really need it.

What do you get if you cross a book with a pencil?

A scolding from the librarian.

Kyle: My teacher is really dumb.
Lyle: What gives you that idea?
Kyle: He spends the whole day asking everybody questions.

Teacher: You cannot sleep in class.
Student: I could if everyone were a little more quiet.

Knock, knock.
Who's there?
Quentin.
Quentin who?
Quentin Rome, do as the Romans do.

Hotel Guest: Please give me a room and a bath.
Clerk: I can give you the room, but you'll have to take your own bath.

April Fooler—Invisible Gum

To prepare: Hide a well-chewed piece of bubble gum in your mouth. Don't let anybody know it's there.

Tell a friend you found some amazing gum. Say the gum is invisible until you chew it. Your friend won't believe you, of course. Tell your friend you can prove it. Hold out your empty palm and say, "I have these two pieces left."

Pretend to unwrap one piece of the "invisible gum." Pretend to pop it into your mouth. Start chewing the real gum. When it's just right, blow a bubble and say, "See?"

Hold out your open hand. Offer your last piece of "invisible gum" to your friend. Say, "Here, you try it." Pretend to drop the "gum." Look around for a minute. Then shrug your shoulders and say, "If you can find it, you can have it."

Man in Rowboat: If dams hold up rivers, what
    holds up banks?
Man in Raft: Robbers.

Little Brother: What would you do if we were
    attacked by killer tomatoes?
Big Sister: I'd fight them off with a salad
    shooter.

Rider: I would like to rent a horse.
Renter: How long?
Rider: As long as you've got. There will be five
of us.

Why do elephants have ivory tusks?
Iron tusks would rust.

What do you get if you cross a dentist with the Tooth Fairy?
  A mouth full of quarters.

Mother: What's taking you so long to put on
    your shoes?
Daughter: They're pointed.
Mother: What difference does that make?
Daughter: They're pointed in the wrong
    direction.

Knock, knock.
Who's there?
Carey.
Carey who?
Carey the groceries in.

Why were the Dark Ages so confusing?
  They were the days of the knights.

Ice Queen: What kind of party should we give at
    the Winter Palace?
Ice King: A snow ball would be nice.

Knock, knock.
Who's there?
Ardly.
Ardly who?
Ardley made any noise.

Biff: Ouch! I just got a lump on the head.
Boff: That's swell.

Grocery Shopper: This cabbage is flat.
Vegetable Clerk: Wait and I'll get a cabbage
     patch.

Rancher: If cowboys ride horses, what do you
     call someone who rides cows?
Farmer: Weird.

Knock, knock.
Who's there?
Wilfred.
Wilfred who?
Wilfred come out?

What do you get when you cross a cat with a
lemon?
   A sour puss.

Knock, knock.
Who's there?
Sherwood.
Sherwood who?
Sherwood like to be invited in.

Woman in Pet Shop: Does this canary sing?
Pet Shop Owner: No. It just sits around making
    bird calls.

Mother: Where's the cat?
Son: I mailed it like you said.
Mother: I didn't tell you to mail it.
Son: You said to put the cat in the kitty letter
box.

Arctic Explorer: What animals are we likely to
see at the North Pole?
Eskimo Guide: Polar bears and pole cats.

Knock, knock.
Who's there?
Sherlock.
Sherlock who?
Sherlock the door?

Why are books about spirits hard to read?
Ghostwriters write them in invisible ink.

What did the clock say to the watch?
Tock to you later.

What's a walnut?
Somebody who's crazy about walls.

Little Willy caught a pig.
He dressed it in a bright red wig.
Willy's pig was not a fool.
He sits in front of me at school.

Knock, knock.
Who's there?
Watkin.
Watkin who?
Watkin I tell you? It's me.

Bragging Billy: I can say 12 o'clock backwards
as fast as I can say it forwards.
Doubting Tom: Prove it.
Bragging Billy: Noon. Noon.

Why do elephants have wrinkled knees?
They get them from scrubbing floors.

Knock, knock.
Who's there?
Ramsay.
Ramsay who?
Ramsay baaaaaaaaaa!

Fern: What would you do if you were the last
　　　person on earth?
Fawn: I'd stop waiting for the phone to ring.

Arnold: What is the heaviest thing in the world?
Atlas: A pizza with everything on it.

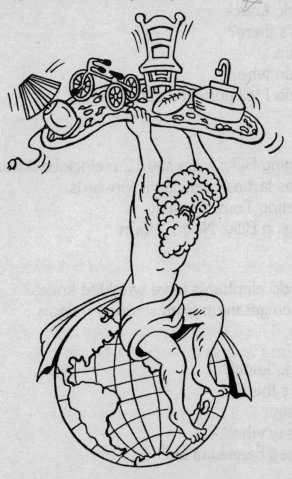

Man in Shoe Store: Do you sell running shoes?
Clerk: No. They're all sitting quietly in their
    boxes.

Ghost Guest: How do you make your haunted
    house so noisy?
Ghost Host: I put on lots of scream doors and
    windows.

Waiter: The customer sent these pancakes back
    because they look terrible.
Chef: Put a little pancake make-up on them and
    take them back.

Dad: Where's tonight's paper?
Mom: I wrapped the garbage in it and threw it
    out.
Dad: I wanted to see it.
Mom: There wasn't much to see. Only a banana
    peel and some coffee grounds.

Patient: I feel sick. When is the best time to see
    the doctor?
Nurse: When he's in.

Knock, knock.
Who's there?
Leif.
Leif who?
Leif me alone.

Waiter (*to rabbit in restaurant*): What would you like to eat?
Rabbit: I'd like a big helping of lettuce, carrots, spinach and potatoes.
Waiter (*to lion sitting with rabbit*): And what would you like, sir?
Lion: Nothing, thank you. I'll just wait for the rabbit to finish.

If peanut butter is such a great invention, why does it stick to the roof of your mouth?

What do you get if you cross an alligator with a hummingbird?
   A mosquito that really bites!

Customer in Restaurant: This water tastes like fruit juice.
Waiter: I'm not surprised. It comes from the grape lakes.

34

Knock, knock.
Who's there?
Oswald.
Oswald who?
Oswald my bubble gum.

Knock, knock.
Who's there?
Harvey.
Harvey who?
Harvey going to wait out here all day?

What can a canary do that an elephant can't?
Take a bath in a saucer.

Knock, knock.
Who's there?
Reade.
Reade who?
Reade my lips.

Mrs. Frankenstein: Did you change the baby,
    dear?
Dr. Frankenstein: What should I change it into?

Lady Diner: Pardon me, but do you have frog's
     legs?
Waiter: Yes. And the cook has chicken wings.

Knock, knock.
Who's there?
Wynn.
Wynn who?
Wynn a few, lose a few.

Knock, knock.
Who's there?
Vincent.
Vincent who?
Vincent me. Let me in.

Knock, knock.
Who's there?
Windsor.
Windsor who?
Windsor blowing hard. Let me in.

Why do elephants have trunks?
They'd look silly with glove compartments.

Knock, knock.
Who's there?
Yul.
Yul who?
Yul be sorry if you don't let me in.

Why don't elephants forget?
Elephants have nothing to remember.

Where do you find elephants?
Very close to where you lost them.

Bubba: Dad! Hurry to the grocery store and
then come home right away! The house is
on fire!
Dad: Why do I have to stop at the grocery
store?
Bubba: Marshmallows!

Peter: Mommy, all the kids at school call me a
werewolf.
Mother: Never mind them. Now comb your face
and run outside and play.

Aunty: My goodness. How does your mother
keep your clothes so clean?
Junior: She doesn't let me wear them.

Aunty: And what does your family eat for
breakfast?
Junior: Toast and marmalade.
Aunty (*serving toast and marmalade*): Why
aren't you eating your toast and
marmalade?
Junior: I don't eat it at home, either.

38

Farmer Jones: Which weeds grow fastest?
Farmer MacDonald: The ones that grow by the
    yard.

What has 50 legs and goes hop hop hop hop
hop?
    Half a centipede.

April Fooler—The Super-gravity Spot

Tell a friend you know a place where it is impossible to stand without falling down. Your friend will want to know where it is.

Slowly walk along a wall. Any wall will do. Act very seriously. Study the wall as if you were looking for a special place. Feel it with your hands. Put your ear against the wall and "listen."

When your friend's curiosity can't stand any more, shout, "Here it is! This is a super-gravity spot."

Tell your friend to stand sideways against the wall at the spot you picked. The foot and shoulder of one side must touch the wall. Stand back. Warn your friend by saying, "The super-gravity will take effect when I count to three. When I reach three, raise the leg that is not touching the wall. Be ready to fall down." Count out loud to three and say, "Raise your leg—*now!*"

Your friend will not be able to stand on your "super-gravity" spot. Try it for yourself.

Monster Teacher: Ooops! My glass eye rolled under my desk.
Monster Principal: Don't tell me you lost another pupil.

Knock, knock.
Who's there?
Adair.
Adair who?
Adair you to open this door.

Aunty: My, you've grown up since I saw you last.
Kid: It's the only way I know how to grow.

Tad: What makes you think the new kid is tough?
Brad: He flosses his teeth with barbed wire.

Kid: Good news, dad. You promised me 50 cents for every "A" I got in school, remember?
Dad: I sure do. What's the good news?
Kid: I just saved you ten dollars. I got all "Fs."

Knock, knock.
Who's there?
Mable.
Mable who?
Mable Syrup.

Knock, knock.
Who's there?
Turner.
Turner who?
Turner handle and let me in.

Sheriff: Did you hear about the family of
thieves?
Deputy: What did they do?
Sheriff: The father took the bus, the mother
took a bath, the daughter took a walk and
the son took his time.

Mavis: I have two hobbies.
Lois: What are they?
Mavis: One is my flea circus. The other is
scratching.

Bart: Why are you watching the escalator?
Clyde: I'm waiting for my gum to come back.

Man: Why does this shirt collar feel so tight?
Salesman: Your head is through the buttonhole,
  sir.

Knock, knock.
Who's there?
Anita.
Anita who?
Anita use the phone.

Doctor: I'm afraid your baby swallowed a frog.
Mother: Oh, dear, how is he?
Doctor: I won't know until he stops hopping.

Rich Uncle: Money isn't everything.
Poor Nephew: I know, but right now it's all I
    need.

Teacher: Herky, describe a skeleton.
Herky: Bones with the people scraped off.

Knock, knock.
Who's there?
Osborn.
Osborn who?
Osborn in August.

Grandma: Did the sweater I made for you fit like
    a glove?
Jarvis: Yes, the sleeves cover my hands.

Waiter: Would you like a sharper knife to cut your meat?
Diner: No, but a chain saw might help.

Diner (*finishing sandwich*): Waiter! There's no meat in this sandwich!
Waiter: You must have missed it. It was right under the pickle slice.

Teacher: Well, Sean, are you learning something today?
Sean: No. I'm listening to you.

Knock, knock.
Who's there?
Roarke.
Roarke who.
Roarke, roarke, I'm a frog.

Jeff: Is a gallon of ice cream very much?
Tyrone: It depends if you're buying it or eating it.

What's as big as an elephant but doesn't weigh anything?
Its shadow.

Teacher: Johnny, wake up Billy.
Johnny: You wake him up. You put him to
    sleep.

Knock, knock.
Who's there?
Rubin.
Rubin who?
Rubin keeping me waiting long enough.

Mike: Has anybody seen my baseball cap?
Pete: It's on your head.
Mike: Phew! I'm glad you told me or I'd have
    gone home without it.

Fenn: Teacher thinks I'm a perfect idiot.
Finn: Well, she's wrong. Nobody's perfect.

Tour Guide: This castle has not been touched in
    500 years. Everything is just where it was
    when the knights left for war.
Cuthbert: Just like my room when I leave for
    school.

Knock, knock.
Who's there?
Dawn.
Dawn who?
Dawnkey. Hee haw.

Teacher: Why were you late this morning?
Werner: The sign said, "School, go slow."

Eye Doctor: Read the letters on that chart.
Maribelle: What chart?

Knock, knock.
Who's there?
Toby.
Toby who?
Toby or not to be.

Willa: You're wearing one red sock and one
green one.
Wanda: Gee, I've got another pair just like it at
home.

Fisherman (*on dock*): You've been watching me
fish for three hours. Do you want to try?
Man: No, thanks. I don't have the patience.

An apple a day keeps the doctor away. What keeps the dentist away?

Bad breath.

How can you tell if there's an elephant in the refrigerator?

The door won't close.

Knock, knock.
Who's there?
Val.
Val who?
Val, what are you waiting for? Let me in.

New Ghost: Will I be safe in this graveyard?
Old Ghost: Of course. We're protected by the
    ghost guard.

Knock, knock.
Who's there?
Kipp.
Kipp who?
Kipp on knockin'.

Myra (*running out of house with bag of
    garbage*): Am I too late for the garbage?
Garbage man: Nope. Jump right in.

Kim (*rushing into principal's office*): Mrs. Willis!
    Come quickly!
Principal: Have a seat. You'll just have to wait
    your turn.
Principal (*much later*): Thank you for waiting,
    Kim. What is it?
Kim: The school is on fire.

Knock, knock.
Who's there?
Sara.
Sara who?
Sara doctor in the house? These jokes are sick.

Mom: Why is Junior having so much trouble
    learning to ride his bike?
Dad: The road doesn't turn when he does.

Kirby: I don't deserve a zero for my homework.
Teacher: I know, but it's the lowest grade I can
    give.

Darby: How long before my birthday?
Mom: Why do you want to know?
Darby: I want to know when to start being
    good.

Knock, knock.
Who's there?
Wanda.
Wanda who?
Wanda why nobody opens the door?

April Fooler—Monster paper

To prepare: Place a small scrap of smudged, old-looking paper in a small envelope.

Tell a friend you have a piece of ancient paper from a mummy's tomb. Slowly open the envelope. Let your friend peek inside. Tell your friend not to touch the paper because something *terrible* could happen.

When your friend asks what could happen, say you will demonstrate. Carefully take the paper from the envelope between your thumb and forefinger. Hold it in front of your friend's face. Say very seriously, "Don't say I didn't warn you."

Grip the paper tightly with the thumbs and forefingers of both hands. Hold the paper at arm's length. Turn your head sideways as if the paper could explode. Ask your friend, "Are you ready?" Wait for a moment as if you're afraid of what will happen. Then say, "Here goes!"

Quickly tear the paper in half. Hold up the two pieces and say, "See? It really is *tear*-able."

Knock, knock.
Who's there?
York.
York who?
York, york, york. This is funny.

How do you know peanuts are fattening?
Did you ever see a skinny elephant?

When is it dangerous to stand in a puddle up to your toes?
When you're standing on your head.

Herky: Mommy! Mommy! I just had a scary
    dream about vampires!
Herky's Mother: Oh, dear! Not another
    bitemare.

Teacher: Name five things that contain milk.
Farmer's son: Three cows and two goats.

Knock, knock.
Who's there?
Wade.
Wade who?
Wade a minute.

Teacher: Were you copying Welby's paper?
Chuck: No, I was only looking to see if he
    copied mine right.

Customer (*in grocery store*): Does the manager
    know you knocked over this whole pile of
    canned tomatoes?
Stock Boy: I think so. He's underneath.

April Fooler—Face It

To prepare: Have two sheets of blank paper, three pencils and a watch or clock with a second hand ready.

Say to a friend, "I can draw more different faces with one hand in one minute than you can. You can use two hands if you like."

When your friend accepts the challenge, hand over one sheet of paper and two pencils. Turn your backs so neither can see what the other is drawing.

Put the clock or watch in plain sight. Say the contest will begin when the second hand reaches 12. When it does, say, "Start!"

Begin drawing *clock* faces as fast as you can. Just draw circles. Don't bother to put in any numbers. Draw only one *clock hand* in each circle. Draw each hand in a slightly different position around the dial.

Your friend will probably run out of faces after drawing happy, sad, mad and frowning faces. Remember to shout "Fooled you!" when you show your "faces."

TICK
TOCK

Aunty: Are you a good student, Irwin?
Irwin: Yes, and no.
Aunty: What do you mean, yes and no?
Irwin: I mean, yes, I am no good.

Knock, knock.
Who's there?
Zenda.
Zenda who?
Zenda somebody to open the door.

Tourist: How can you tell if the elephants are around?
Zookeeper: I sniff the air for peanut breath.

Teacher: Why is your writing so hard to read?
Leif: To hide my bad spelling.

Knock, knock.
Who's there?
Sloane.
Sloane who?
Sloane Ranger.

Parent: Herbert may be a little dull today. He
 has a cold in his head.
Teacher: Thank goodness he has something in
 there.

Knock, knock.
Who's there?
Eileen.
Eileen who?
Eileen over and fall down.

Sally: Why does Joe look so weird?
Silly: The doctor gave him a funny look when
 he was born.

Why are ghost psychiatrists so busy?
 Their patients are not all there.

Bragging Ghost: We're special because we can
 walk through walls.
Proud Person: So can we. We just open the
 door first.

The sign was clear as it could be;
It said: "Do not sit beneath this coconut tree."
Willie laughed at such advice.
Now his head is bandaged nice.

April Fooler—Mini-Ghost

To prepare. Hide a clean, white paper tissue in your pocket.

Ask a friend if he or she would like to see a ghost. The answer is sure to be yes.

Make up a scary story. Say you were walking by a graveyard and you saw a tiny ghost. Say you caught it. Your friend won't believe you. Say you can prove it.

Turn around so your friend can't see what you're doing. Take the tissue from your pocket. Drape it over the middle finger of your left hand so it looks like a tiny "ghost." Cup your hands together with the "ghost" finger standing in the middle.

Face your friend. Quickly thrust your cupped hands forward. Wiggle the "ghost" finger. Shout, "BOO!"

61

Ghost pilots (*on their way to wash their sheets*): Off we go into the wild blue launder.

What's worse than a giraffe with a sore throat?
  An elephant with a runny nose.

Knock, knock.
Who's there?
Udell.
Udell who?
Udell me one more knock knock joke and I'm leaving.